Cliff Hanger

JEAN CRAIGHEAD GEORGE

Cliff Hanger

WENDELL MINOR

HARPERCOLLINSPUBLISHERS

Axel washed his tin cup at the hand pump outside the Teton Mountains Climbing School hut and looked up. A storm cloud darkened Death Canyon. Lightning flashed. Axel was glad he wasn't rock climbing now.

"Axel!"

Two mountain climbers ran down the trail. "Your dog
followed us up the mountain," one of the women said.
"We had to leave him at the top of Cathedral Wall."

"You left Grits?" Axel was upset.

"That storm's bad," she said, looking over her shoulder.
"We had to get out of there."

Axel's father, Dag, the leader of the school, heard the news.
He closed the registration book and stepped outside.

Lightning exploded.

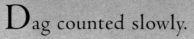Dag counted slowly.

". . . thirty-eight, thirty-nine, forty . . ."

Kaboom, drummed the thunder.

"A mile for every five counts," Dag said. "The storm's eight miles away. We've got enough time to get Grits."

Dag put on his belt, which jangled with climbing nuts and carabiners, and shouldered his rope and backpack.

Axel looked at his dad. "Thanks," he said, and put on his own mountain-climbing gear.

Axel and Dag trekked steadily up the wooded trails, climbed over rock avalanches, and finally arrived at the bottom of the shaft of rock that is Cathedral Wall. A lightning bolt split open the black cloud.

"One, two, three . . ."

Kaboom.

"The storm's only a half mile away," Dag said. "Too close. We'd better wait it out here."

From high on the wall came a howl. Axel looked up.

"Look! Grits got down to Monkey Ledge. If he tries to come on down, he'll fall. Let's go."

"No," said Dag. "We can't make that climb. It's too difficult. We'll go back to the trail split and up the ridge."

"That'll take too long," Axel said. "I can do it." He tied the rope to his belt and placed his foot in a crack. He reached up.

Dag had no choice. His son was climbing. He picked up the top coil of Axel's rope and took a deep breath.

"Think out your moves," he said, wrapping the rope around his waist and bracing his foot against a rock.

"On belay," he called out.

"Climbing!" Axel answered.

Axel climbed slowly, from crack to crack to ledge to crack, moving like a ballet dancer. His father let out rope as he climbed.

When Axel was fifteen feet up, he jammed a climber's nut securely into a crack. He clipped a carabiner into the nut, and his rope in the carabiner. He relaxed. If he fell now, the nut, the carabiner, and his dad would stop him from plunging to his death. He climbed on.

Axel looked up. Grits was crouched on the ledge, about to jump to him. "Stay!" Axel yelled.

Splats of rain hit the wall. Axel climbed very carefully. Using the tips of his fingers and the edges of his climbing shoes, he pulled himself upward until his hand found the rim of Monkey Ledge. The next move was dangerous. Climbers had fallen here.

Thinking clearly, Axel placed both hands firmly on the ledge and concentrated. Slowly he pressed on them. His body rose. When his arms were straight, he placed his right foot beside his right hand, then his left foot beside his left hand.

Bent like a hairpin, he found his balance and stood up. Grits wagged his tail but did not move. He was scared.

Lightning buzzed across the sky.

"One . . ."

KABOOM. Grits shivered.

"A quarter mile away."

Axel put a nut and carabiner in the wall and roped himself to them. He sat down beside Grits and breathed a sigh of relief. Grits was safe.

Axel picked up his little dog and hugged him.

The cloud opened, and rain poured down. Grits whimpered.

"It's all right," Axel whispered into his fur. "It's all right."

The sky flashed. *KABOOM!*

"No count," said Axel. "It's here, Grits. We're right in the center of the storm." Crackling electricity lifted the hair straight up on Axel's head and arms. The air hummed. Sparks snapped from his ears to the rocks.

He hugged Grits closer.

*F*lash.

". . . seven, eight, nine, ten . . ."

Kaboom.

"Two miles," said Axel. "The storm's going away."

Axel took a dog harness from his pocket and slipped it over Grits's head and shoulders.

The rain stopped. The sun came out. Axel picked up Grits and eased him over the edge of the ledge. Grits clawed the air.

"Dog on belay!" he called to his dad. Slowly Axel let out the rope, lowering Grits down through space.

"Got him!" Dag finally shouted, and looked up. "Axel," he shouted, "when you double your rope to rappel, you'll only have enough rope to get halfway down."

"I know it, but it's okay. I see a good ledge where the rope will end."

Axel wrapped the rope around an outcrop and clipped it to his harness. Then he put his back to the void and leaned out. Holding one end of the rope, letting out the other, he jumped out, dropped, caught himself, jumped out, dropped, caught himself.

And then he came to the end of the rope.

The planned route was still ten feet below.

Dag saw the problem. He studied the wall.

"If you can swing out to your left," he said quietly, "you'll find a good route."

Axel swung across the face of the wall. He reached but could not find a handhold near the route. He swung back. Dag foresaw a disaster.

"Stay where you are," he said. "I'm going for help."

"It'll be too dark," Axel answered. "I'll try again."

Axel ran like a track star back and forth across the vertical wall, back and forth. He swung wider and wider. When he was over Dag's route, he jammed his fist in a crack. He did not swing back.

Axel forced his toes into another crack. When he was secure and firmly balanced, he untied the rope from his waist, pulled it from the boulder on Monkey Ledge, and let it fall to his dad.

No nut, carabiner, or rope was there to save him if he made a mistake. From this moment on, he must free climb.

He began his descent.

Dag watched. The old pro said not one word, for fear of breaking his son's concentration.

When Axel was three feet from the ground, he whooped and jumped down to his father.

"Did it!"

"That was so close, I can't talk about it," Dag said. There was a flash in the canyon. Axel hugged Grits.

". . . twenty-one, twenty-two, twenty-thr—" *Kaboom!*

"The storm's at the hut," Dag said. "Let's wait it out here. I'm beat." He lit his small gas stove and made soup with clear stream water and instant mix. He poured some into a cup for Axel.

"I'll bet Grits sleeps well tonight," Dag said when he finally relaxed. "He was one scared dog."

"I don't know about Grits," Axel answered. "But I was sure scared. I thought I had lost my friend forever."

To Scotty Craighead
—J.C.G.

To all the incredible Craigheads
—W.G.M.

Cliff Hanger
Text copyright © 2002 by Julie Productions Inc.
Illustrations copyright © 2002 by Wendell Minor
Printed in the U.S.A. All rights reserved.
www.harperchildrens.com

Library of Congress Cataloging-in-Publication Data
George, Jean Craighead.
Cliff Hanger / by Jean Craighead George / illustrations by Wendell Minor.—1st ed.
p.   cm.
Summary: Despite the dangers of a thunderstorm, Axel and his father make a difficult climb to rescue Axel's stranded dog.
ISBN 0-06-000260-3—ISBN 0-06-000261-1 (lb)
[1. Rock climbing—Fiction.   2. Dogs—Fiction.   3. Father and sons—Fiction.]
I. Minor, Wendell, ill.   II. Title.
PZ7.G2933 CI 2002   2001024595
[E]—dc21

Typography by Wendell Minor and Al Cetta
1 2 3 4 5 6 7 8 9 10
❖
First Edition